Richard Harding Davis

Dr. Jameson's Raiders vs. the Johannesburg Reformers

Richard Harding Davis

Dr. Jameson's Raiders vs. the Johannesburg Reformers

ISBN/EAN: 9783337298289

Printed in Europe, USA, Canada, Australia, Japan

Cover: Foto ©Andreas Hilbeck / pixelio.de

More available books at **www.hansebooks.com**

DR. JAMESON'S RAIDERS

DR. JAMESON AND HIS OFFICERS RETURNING TO ENGLAND
AS PRISONERS ON BOARD S.S. VICTORIA

DR. JAMESON'S RAIDERS

VS.

THE JOHANNESBURG REFORMERS

BY

RICHARD HARDING DAVIS

FELLOW OF THE ROYAL GEOGRAPHICAL SOCIETY ; AUTHOR OF
"THE PRINCESS ALINE," "THREE GRINGOS IN VENEZUELA
AND CENTRAL AMERICA," "THE RULERS OF THE
MEDITERRANEAN," "GALLAGHER," ETC.

PUBLISHED BY ROBERT HOWARD RUSSELL
AT THE CORNER OF ROSE AND DUANE STREETS
IN THE CITY OF NEW YORK

1897

Dr. Jameson's Raiders

ON the day that Dr. Jameson and his officers were found guilty of infringing the Foreign Enlistment act and sent to Holloway Prison, Mr. John Hays Hammond, the American engineer, who was a most active member of the Reform Committee in Johannesburg at the time of the raid, was staying in London at the Savoy Hotel. I happened to hear this, and remembering that Mr. Hammond had been one of those who invited Jameson to enter Johannesburg, and who had then left him to fight his way there unsupported, said that if I had to choose I would rather be in Holloway with Jameson than in the Savoy with Hammond.

This remark was carried to Mr. Hammond by a mutual friend, who asked me to keep my opinion in abeyance until I had heard Hammond's side of the story. The same mutual friend then invited me to dine with Hammond and himself, and for the first time I was told the story of the Jameson raid in such a manner as convinced me that the charges of cowardice laid against the Reform Committee were unmerited. The story, as told to me, is full of interest, putting many things in a new light, adjusting the blame more evenly, and, in my mind at least, removing the charge of lack of faith under which the members of the Reform Committee and the people of Johannesburg have been resting in silence. That they were silent for so long is because they did not wish anything to appear in print while Dr. Jameson was awaiting trial, which might deprive him of the popular sympathy he enjoyed during that period, and which, they hoped, might help to lessen the severity of his sentence. That sentence has now been passed, without much regard having been shown for the point of view of the populace, and Dr. Jameson has paid for his adventure like a man.

As he has had his turn, it seems only right now that he should give place in the public eye to those who have suffered as well as himself, and through his action, whose plans he spoiled and whose purposes his conduct entirely misrepresented to the world. For these other men of the Reform Committee have lain, owing to him, in a far worse jail than Holloway, and some still lie there, some have been sentenced to death, while others have been fined fortunes, and, more than all else besides, they have had to bear the odium of having been believed, both in the United States and in England, to have shown the white feather in deserting a comrade, and of failing to keep the promises of help they had held out to him.

On the other hand, it is not fair to put the Reformers in the light of turning on a man when he is down, or making a scapegoat of Dr. Jameson. Dr. Jameson could have cleared them from all responsibility for his act before going to jail, and he did not. He could have said then that he entered the Transvaal not only at his own risk, but against their expressed wishes and entreaties, and, though they wrote to him before he was imprisoned, and pointed out to him that they were lying under a heavy burden of blame which he could remove if he wished, he did not answer their letters.

My authority for what I am now relating does not come only from members of the Reform Committee, but from friends of Dr. Jameson also: those who rode at his side when he made his armed invasion of the Transvaal and those who knew him in London and who visit him now that he is in prison. Dr. Jameson himself I have only met once, but I have had access to the green book of the South African Republic, and to the blue book of the Cape Colony; I was present both at the preliminary proceedings against Dr. Jameson and his officers at the Bow Street Police Court, and at the formal trial before the Lord Chief Justice; I have seen the cipher dispatches of the reformers the daily papers published at Johannesburg at the time of the raid, and I have been told the story again and again from every point of view,

and heard it told to others by the men who were the
leaders in the revolution.

The Reform Committee of Johannesburg was organized with the object of obtaining certain reforms for
abuses which had grown so serious that the position of
the Uitlanders in the Transvaal had become unbearable.
There is an objection which is instantly raised whenever
the condition of the Uitlanders is described as I have just
stated it, and it is this: "If the Uitlanders did not like
the laws of the Transvaal why did they not leave it and
go elsewhere; the world is large enough for everybody?
Why did they instead plot to upset the Government of
the Boers who had sheltered them, and who only asked
to be left to breed their cattle and to farm their ranches
in peace?" The answer to this very fair question is that
the laws to which the Reform Committee objected did
not exist when the majority of its members had entered
the Transvaal eight years before.

At that time the revenue of the country was barely
able to support it, and immigrants were warmly wel-
comed. The law as it then stood was that a Uitlander
could obtain full rights of citizenship after a residence
of five years, and with this understanding many Americans and Englishmen bought land in the Transvaal,
built houses, and brought their families to live in them,
invested their capital in mines and machinery, and gradu-
ally severed the ties that had bound them to the rest of
the world. But when the gold seekers grew into a majority, the Boer, who still retained his love for pastoral
and agricultural pursuits, passed a new law, which declared that the Uitlander could not obtain the franchise
until he had first renounced his allegiance to any other
country, and then, after a lapse of eight or fifteen years
he could, if it pleased the Government, become a burgher,
with a right to vote; but that, if it did not please the
Government he could never hope to become a citizen of
the Transvaal. In other words, the Uitlander was asked
to give up what rights he had as a citizen of the United
States or of Great Britain on the chance that in fifteen

years he might become a citizen of the country, toward
the support of which he paid eighteen-twentieths of the
revenue, in which his children had been born, and in
which he had made his home, but in the meanwhile he
would be a man without a country and with no Government to which he could turn for help or to which he
could look to redress a wrong. This uncertainty of obtaining the franchise was the chief grievance.

There were many other grievances, and they are so well
known that they are described as the "admitted grievances." When the Uitlander first came to the Transvaal, the revenue of the country was $375,000; it is now
$10,000,000, and, as I have said, the Uitlander finds
eighteen-twentieths of that total revenue, and yet it has
been practically impossible for him to obtain even an
education for his children in the state schools which his
money supported. The sale of monopolies by the Government to different companies made his expenses ex-
cessive beyond reason, and the mismanagement of the
railroads led to delay in the transportation of machinery
and of perishable goods, which robbed legitimate business of any profit. Another evil arose from the Liquor
Trust, which gave the complete control of all the liquor
sold on the Rand into the hands of one firm, which
manufactured a poisonous quality of whisky, and sold it
without restriction to the natives, upon whom the mines
depended for labor, and who for half the time were in-
capacitated from attending to the work which they were
paid to do. Land that had been sold to the Uitlanders
for mining purposes was not regarded by the Boer Government as their private property. This being the case,
the Polish Jews, who handled most of the liquor sold on
the Rand, were able to place their canteens where they
pleased, at the very mouth of a shaft if they wished to do
so, with the result that the Kafir boys were constantly
drinking, and in consequence as constantly falling into
open shafts, fighting among themselves, and suffering
from the most serious accidents.

Edgar P. Rathbone, late Mining Inspector of the east

and central districts of the Witwatersrand under the Boer
Government, said in a recent interview of this grievance:
" Every Monday morning, when the natives have to go
to work after their pay day, one-third of the men are
laid off drunk. If they are apparently sober enough to
be able to travel down the main ladderways and to go
into the cages, as soon as they get under ground the different atmosphere utterly unfits them for work. The
white miner runs a risk under the mining regulations in
having a drunken Kafir at work in the mine, and he is
forced to send such a man to the surface again. In my
own experience I have frequently had to order natives
out of the mines because they were quite unfit to be
intrusted with drilling or any other work. You must
also remember that it is impossible to examine, or even
to distinguish, every case of drunkenness among some
hundreds or thousands of Kafirs, and thus men who are
at least partially under the influence of drink are allowed
to go about their work in the mine. I have no hesita-
tion in saying that a large proportion of the many fear-
ful accidents which happen on the Rand are due, directly
or indirectly, to this cause."

Another monopoly under the protection of the Government was the sale of dynamite, which gave one man
exclusive right to manufacture that most essential part
of a miner's supplies on the condition that he would
manufacture it in the Transvaal. He did not manufacture it in the Transvaal, but bought a low quality of dynamite in Germany, changed the wrappers in his so-called
manufactory, and sold the stuff at any price he pleased.
It is said that the accidental explosions which have occurred in the Rand are largely due to the low quality of
this dynamite, which was the only brand the miners were
allowed to use.

The Government's method of protecting the Netherlands Railroad is also interesting; the coal deposits run
parallel with the gold mines, but at a distance of some
ten to thirty miles. This coal could be bought at the
mouth of the shaft by any one for 7s. 6d., but the Nether-

lands Railroad charged from 3d. to 1s. a ton per mile
for carrying it over the few miles intervening between
the gold fields and the gold mines. So that the coal,
which originally sold for 7s. 6d., cost, when delivered at the
mines, from 15s. to 30s. The average charge for freight
per mile in the United States is one-half cent per mile,
in England it is three-quarters of a cent, which throws
a lurid light on what the earnings must have been for
the Netherlands Railroad when it charged from 6 to 24
cents per mile. There was so very little profit in this
for the gold mines that the different companies purchased
strips of land, and, giving each other permission to use
the land already owned, they mapped out a railroad over
which they proposed to carry what coal they needed.
When the Boers heard of this, they passed a law for-
bidding them to build this railroad, and later, when
the miners attempted to carry the coal in ox-carts, with
traction engines, they were forbidden to do that also.
Freight can be sent from the Cape in almost a direct line
by an English railroad which stops at the border of the
Transvaal, the rest of the haul being made over the system of the Netherlands Company. This point of the
border is only forty miles from Johannesburg. Or it
can be taken in a more roundabout way from a point
much further east. If it comes from this direction, it
travels 300 miles instead of forty miles.

In order to make the Uitlanders use the long haul, and
so bring more money into the coffers of the Government railroad, the Netherlands Company allowed the
freight to congest at the point forty miles from Johannesburg, and kept it there for three or four weeks, and sub-
jected it to such delay and to such treatment on the way
up as they hoped would finally drive the Uitlanders into
abandoning the use of the more direct route from the
Cape. Sooner than do this the Uitlanders organized a
system of ox-carts, and started to carry their freight over-
land in that slow and cumbersome fashion. To prevent
their doing this, the Government closed the " drifts," as
the fords of the rivers are called, and so prevented their

PAUL KRUGER

PRESIDENT OF THE SOUTH AFRICAN REPUBLIC

crossing. It required an ultimatum from Great Britain to open them again.

These are a few instances of the laws and customs of a Government which has been seeking sympathy as a free and enlightened republic, and which compares, and not unfavorably, with the free and enlightened republics of Central America.

The spirit of discontent caused by these grievances grew slowly, and showed itself when it first found expression in the form of perfectly constitutional agitations. In May, 1894, 13,000 Uitlanders petitioned the Volksraad for the rights of the franchise, and it is on record in the minutes of that legislative body that this petition was received with jeers and laughter. That in itself was not soothing to the petitioners, especially as it came from the representatives of those of the inhabitants who were in the minority, for even at that time the Uitlanders greatly outnumbered the original settlers of the Transvaal. Two months later another petition, signed this time by 32,500 inhabitants, was received by the Volksraad in the same manner, one of its members, indeed, going so far as to rise and say: " If you want the franchise, why don't you fight for it?"

His invitation was accepted later, when the inhabitants of Johannesburg, finding there was no help to be obtained through the " sacred right of petition," organized the Reform Committee and prepared themselves to take what they wanted by a revolution and the use of arms. I am not pretending here to defend the revolutionists; I only wish to tell what led up to the Jameson raid, and to show that, no matter what the Reform Committee have done or wished to do as revolutionists, they were at least not faithless to Jameson, who became one of their own party, and who was one of their friends.

No one denies that their purpose was to change the laws of the country, or that they smuggled arms into Johannesburg to accomplish that purpose, if it could not be accomplished by any other means. But that they intended to upset the republic, I do not believe any more than I believe that they intended to turn the Transvaal into a British dependency, or to raise the British flag, as it was repeatedly stated at the time they had meant to do.

One difficulty in dealing with the history of this revolution lies in the fact that, while the men in it had the same end in view, they were working toward that end with different motives. There were a great many men in our War of the Rebellion who fought for the dollars they received for fighting, as they to-day fight for pensions, and there were a great many contractors who made money out of the war, but no one would argue from that that all the other men in it held low motives, or that the cause for which they fought was not a great one. There is an element in the affair of the Transvaal which can only be described as the unknown quantity, and that element is, of course, Mr. Cecil Rhodes. That he would have been benefited by a reform in the laws of the Transvaal is well understood, but so would have every one else who was interested in the mines there, and who was hampered by the restrictions, taxes and monopolies, which added a burden of expense to every ton of ore that was taken out of the ground. Cecil Rhodes, as one of those largely interested, was proportionately interested in seeing labor made cheaper, transportation made easier, and those men in office who were interested in the mines, instead of the Boers, who were not. As a matter of fact, Mr. Cecil Rhodes' interest in the Consolidated Gold Fields was but one-fifteenth of its profits, so it was not money, but the development of his cherished plan for a combination of all of the South African Republics that moved him. What he hoped from the revolution we can imagine; that he would have looked at a change of government in the Transvaal as another step toward the unification of all the republics in South Africa is most probable, and he knew that to such a union the Boers of themselves would never consent. But that the whole revolution was a plot to seize the Transvaal for the sake of its gold mines and for the aggrandizement of Great

Britain, and that the men of the Reform Committee who
risked their lives in the cause of revolution were the
puppets of Rhodes, moving at his bidding, is absurd.
There were other big men in the revolution besides
Cecil Rhodes, and it was perfectly well agreed among
these men that no flag but that of the Transvaal Republic was to be raised when the revolution began, and whatever the Englishmen may have wished, the Germans,
Afrikanders and those of the Boers who were in sympathy with the revolution, and the Americans, which latter composed one-sixth of the Reform Committee,
formed a majority which certainly had no intention of
turning the country over to the Queen, and, as a matter
of history, the Transvaal flag floated over the Gold
Fields building, which was the headquarters of the
revolutionists, from the first to the last. Personally, I
am convinced, after having talked with the men who
were at the head of this revolution, that the greater part
of them as honestly believed that they were acting for
the best good of the country in trying to overthrow the
Boer Government, as did the revolutionists of 1776 in
our own country, or as do the rebels in Cuba at the
present day.

Six weeks before the Jameson raid the Reform Committee had mapped out their plan of action. They had
spent £70,000 ($350,000) in provisions, which they ex-
pected would outlast a two months' siege; they had ar-
ranged that the water supply of Johannesburg could not
be cut off from the outside, and they had ordered rifles
and Maxim guns and were smuggling them across the
border. This was the most difficult part of their work,
for guns are as strictly prohibited to Uitlanders in
Johannesburg as are public meetings, and every one who
owned a rifle was a marked man in consequence. It is
well to remember this, for it is not as though Johannesburg in that respect resembled some of our own mining
towns, where weapons are sometimes as plentiful as pick-
axes, and where a call to arms would merely mean the
reading of the payrolls at the shafts of the different mines.

It was while these guns for defense were slowly coming in that Dr. Jameson, the administrator of the Chartered Company's affairs, was told of the movement of the
revolutionists, and asked by them if he would, in case
they needed his assistance, come across the border to the
aid of his fellow-countrymen, bringing with him his
mounted police and 1,500 extra guns, which they would
send him to Mafeking. The gentlemen of the Reform
Committee were Dr. Jameson's personal friends, they
had trekked with him all over the surrounding country,
hunting, prospecting and exploring, they knew he was a
man ready for adventure, and that in the easy spirit of
the unsettled country about them it would not be difficult
for him to gather around him a body of men ready to
follow wherever he led.

Jameson gave his consent readily, and agreed to the
conditions under which he was to enter the Transvaal.
These conditions were exceedingly important and exceedingly explicit; he was to move only when the Reformers gave the signal for him to do so, and they, as the
chief movers in the plot and the men having most at
stake, were to be allowed to judge exactly when that time
had come, or if he should come at all; that when he came
he must bring 1,500 men with him, and the extra 1,500
guns on which they counted. This he promised to do,
and asked in return that they should write him a letter
inviting him to cross the border, which he could show
later as his justification for his action.

The situation at this time was stretched geographically
in the form of a triangle, with three bases of action, all
working to the same end. The members of the Reform
Committee, who were preparing to demand certain reforms and concessions, and ready, if they failed to get
them peaceably, to fight for them, were at Johannesburg;
Dr. Jameson, with his filibusters who were to rush in,
but only when they were wanted and if they were wanted,
was at Pitsanti, in Matabele Land, and Cecil Rhodes, the
unknown quantity, was at the Cape, aiding and advising
them all.

The letter to Jameson was signed by five men, and the date was purposely omitted, so that Jameson could write it in later. These five men were Charles Leonard, a British subject born in Cape Colony, educated at Cambridge, and a prominent lawyer of Johannesburg, where he had a practice which amounted to $50,000 a year; Col. Francis Rhodes, a brother of Cecil Rhodes, and an officer in the English army who has seen service in India and in the Soudan; John Hays Hammond, who, as a mining expert, now commands a salary just twice as large as that of the President of the United States; Lionel Phillips, the largest individual property owner in the Transvaal, and George Farrar, an importing merchant. These men, who, with the exception of Leonard, who escaped to England, were afterward tried by the Government and sentenced to be hanged, were properly described by Jameson as "leading citizens of Johannesburg," as they would have been leading citizens in any community in which they chanced to live.

The contents of their letter to Jameson are well known. As a literary effort intended to plead a certain cause, it does not strike one as a very successful performance, as it does not sound sincere; it shows on its face that it was written for publication, and it has none of the simplicity which as a factor in the conversation of the men who signed it is their most convincing argument. It described the critical state of affairs in Johannesburg, and asked Jameson, " should a disturbance arise," to come to the aid of that city, and expressed fears as to the safety of the "unarmed men, women and children of our race " who were there, in the event of a conflict. It was of this line that Jameson made use when he told his men they were going to protect " women and children," and which the poet laureate embodied in his absurd verses when he wrote:

> " There are girls in the gold reef city
> And mothers and children, too,
> And they cry ' Hurry up, for pity,'
> So what could a brave man do ? "

As this letter was handed to Jameson by the signers six weeks before he made his raid, the idea of the girls of the gold reef city crying " Hurry up, for pity!" during that length of time and his not heeding them, has its humorous side.

During the six weeks which intervened between the delivery of this letter and the raid, the Reform Committee continued actively in its preparation for the defense of the city. Its plan was to declare itself on Jan. 6, 1896. By that time it hoped to have 5,000 rifles, a sufficient number of Maxim guns, and 1,000,000 cartridges hidden away within the limits of Johannesburg and in the surrounding mines; it also counted, with reason, on having control of the forts which covered the city, and which were at that time guarded by a few Boer soldiers, who could have been driven out by assault. The committee relied confidently on the immediate services of at least 20,000 of the inhabitants of Johannesburg and on the help of many who would join them when they saw that it was safe to do so. With these men fully armed, with the town provisioned for a two-months' siege, they felt they would be in a position by Jan. 6 to send their ultimatum to the Government at Pretoria. The conditions of this ultimatum were to be that unless the Boers gave them the reforms for which they had petitioned without success they would, at the end of three days, set up a provisional Government and defend Johannesburg against all comers.

It was then, at this point, when the minds of half the people in the country would be wavering as to whether it was better to join the reformers or to uphold the old régime, that Dr. Jameson was to have come in with his 1,500 police, like a " flying wedge " and bring the wavering ones, both Uitlanders and Boers, from ranches, farms and villages, and deliver this triumphant addition to his own well-organized force into the hands of the provisional Government at Johannesburg. That is what was to have happened. What did happen was this:

On Dec. 25 one of the Reform Committee was sent

Dʀ. L. S. JAMESON, C. B.

in great haste to the Cape to arrange some final details
and to hurry up the arms, which were slow in coming,
and without which the revolution was as formidable in
appearance, but as absolutely impotent in fact, as an
empty dynamite can. When at the Cape this member
discovered a hitch in their plans, and so informed the
Reform Committee, and this caused Samuel Jameson
at Johannesburg to send the following telegram to his
brother at Mafeking:

"It is absolutely necessary to postpone flotation
through unforeseen circumstances here altogether unex-
pected. * * * You must not move until you have
received instructions to."

This was on Dec. 26, just three days before the raid.
On Dec. 27 two telegrams were received in Johannesburg by Jameson's brother to the following effect:

PITSANI, Dec. 27.

Jameson to Jameson:

Dr. Wolff will understand that distant cutting. British Bechuanaland police have already gone forward. Guarantee already
given therefore let J. H. Hammond telegraph instantly all right.

And Dec. 27:

Jameson to Jameson:

Dr. Jameson says he cannot give extension of refusal for flotation for December as Transvaal Boers opposition.

These telegrams were the first intimation the Reform
Committee received that Dr. Jameson had some idea of
taking the bit between his teeth, of dragging the reins
out of their hands, and bolting. Such a contingency had
not occurred to them. They knew he was perfectly well
acquainted with their helpless condition; they knew that
he had been strictly enjoined not to appear on the scene
until Hammond gave him the signal. And at once, in
the greatest possible alarm at the possible failure of their
long-matured plans, they sent two messengers post haste
to warn him not to move from where he was. Major
Heany, an American, a graduate of West Point, and a

*NOTE.—This refers to the cutting of the telegraph wires to
Kimberly.

soldier who has seen service in the Portuguese and Kafir wars, was dispatched by Hammond on a special train, and Edward Holden was sent to Mafeking on horseback. So well did Holden understand the necessity of reaching Jameson in time to head him off that he made the 150 miles between between Johannesburg and Mafeking in seventeen hours, changing his saddle to five different horses. He arrived outside the Jameson headquarters at 4 o'clock on Saturday morning, the 28th of December, where he was met by his friend, Lieut. Grenfell of the Guards, who conducted him to Jameson, to whom he delivered Hammond's message. Heany and his special train arrived later on the 28th, and he handed Jameson his message. On the day previous the following telegram had arrived from Hammond: "Wire just received. Experts report decidedly adverse. I absolutely condemn further developments at present."

This was on Saturday morning, so before Jameson left Pitsani, and long before he had crossed the border of the Transvaal, and long before he had been ordered back by a Commissioner of the Transvaal Republic, and, later, by the representative of the High Commissioner for Great Britain, he had received two special messages from his friends, telling him he was not wanted, and a telegram from a man who was to give him the signal to start, begging him to stay where he was.

In spite of this, on Sunday, Sept. 29, Dr. Jameson started on his ride to Johannesburg against the wishes of Cecil Rhodes and against the entreaties of the Reform Committee, and instead of bringing with him the 1,500 men and the 1,500 extra rifles agreed upon, he came with only 500 men and carried no extra arms.

The story, up to this point, has had to deal almost entirely with the reformers of Johannesburg and their plans; but we must leave them now and take up the tale of Dr. Jameson and his ride, and, if it is to be told intelligently, it should also relate what was done by the representatives of Great Britain at home and in South Africa, and by President Kruger to stop that ride while

it was going forward. The Reform Committee did not
cease from acting at this time, but as it was Dr. Jameson
who dominated their actions, and as it was he who set
Great Britain, Germany and South Africa by the ears,
and caused the cables to burn for five days from Cape
Town to London and from Berlin to San Francisco, it
is proper that he should now take the centre of the stage,
and that his story should be told with all the detail which
so important a foot note to history deserves. The details
themselves, scanty as they are, have been collected with
some difficulty, and have been verified for me by those
who rode at Jameson's side.

On the afternoon of Sunday, Dec. 29, 1895, the men of
the Chartered Company's police, in camp, at Pitsani
Potlugo, were collected by trumpet call on the parade
ground and formed into a square. Dr. Jameson, the
administrator of the company, then read to them the
"women and children" letter, and informed them that
they were going into the Transvaal to the aid of their
fellow countrymen, and assured them that they would
be joined on the way, not only by the Cape Mounted
Rifles, but that they would be met at Krugersdorp by
2,000 of the Uitlanders, who would escort them into
Johannesburg. It was then about 7 o'clock in the evening, and the force at once started, and after riding all
night, arrived at Malman, on the other side of the border,
at 6 o'clock in the morning, where it was met by two
troops of the Bechuanaland Police. This force, under
Col. Raleigh Grey, had left Mafeking at 10 o'clock the
evening before, and had crossed the border before midnight. The combined forces, as they assembled at Malmani, and as they set out together from that point were
composed approximately as follows:

Four troops (A B C D) Matabele Mounted Police, 380 officers
and men.

Two troops (G and K) Bechuanaland Border Police, 120 officers
and men.

Cape Boys and Kafirs who drove Cape carts and ambulances, 70.

One 12½-pounder field piece; two 7-pounder field pieces; 8
Maxim guns; Cape carts and ambulances.

Among the officers were :

Dr. Leander Starr Jameson, administrator of the Chartered Company's Territory.

Major Sir John Christopher Willoughby, military commander.

Col. Raleigh Grey, in command of the Bechuanaland Police.

Colonel, the Hon. Henry White.

Major, the Hon. Robert White.

Major, the Hon. C. J. Coventry.

Major T. B. Stracey.

Howard M. Grenfell, Lieutenant First Life Guards.

Captain Maurice Heaney, late United States Army, Royal Horse Artillery.

Captain Henry Holden.

Charles H. Villiers, Captain, Royal Horse Guards.

Inspector W. H. Barry.

Captain C. L. D. Munroe.

K. Kincaid Smith, Lieutenant Royal Artillery.

A. V. Gosling, Captain Malabele Mounted Police.

William Bodle, Chief Inspector of Police.

Captain Harold Foley, Scott's Guards.

Lawson B. Dykes, Inspector of Police.

J. H. Kennedy, Captain Matabele Mounted Police.

E. C. F. Garraway, Surgeon-Captain Bechuanaland Border Police.

Lesson Hamilton, Surgeon-Captain.

The personnel of this force was strangely varied, its officers held commissions in the most distinguished regiments of Her Majesty's service, and were members of the oldest and most important families in England. Many of them were closely related to people of title, and some had titles of their own, even among the troopers there were "gentleman rankers;" sons of generals and of members of the House of Peers. With them in the ranks were common adventurers and filibusters; men who, for reasons of their own, had sought a change of fortune in the unsettled country north of the Cape, and boys from the counties of England, sons of field laborers and farmers who had already seen a little " help yourself " fighting in the Kafir and Matabele wars, and with them were veterans of the British Army, who had fought in real wars and who had already served under Jameson against Lobengula in Mashonaland.

The column left Malmani with a scouting party riding

well in advance, followed by four troops protected in front and on the flanks by the Maxims, which were carried in Cape carts—two-wheeled wagons with hooded tops. The provisions and ammunition in carts, and the ambulances came next, and a guard of the remaining two troops brought up the rear. I have read eighteen pages of closely printed instructions, detailing the order in which this column was to move, and setting forth the exact distance in feet at which the flanking parties were to ride from the main column when the advance was unimpeded, and how much closer they were to draw when the column was attacked, but what was planned on paper was not carried out on the veldt, and in spite of, or, perhaps, on account of, the abundance of officers, the ride was made from a military point of view in a strangely amateurish fashion, which fills even the civilian mind with wonder. Halts, for instance, were made at places where there was no water and where high hills surrounded the force on every side, and afforded the enemy absolute protection, and places where there was water and fodder laid out in readiness for the horses, in lines, as it is in cavalry barracks, were passed at a gallop. In spite of these blunders in commissariat and the choice of halting places, the speed of the advancing column was well sustained, especially when one remembers that the field pieces and slow-moving ammunition carts set the pace. By adding up the hours and half hours given the men to rest, and the time consumed by enforced pauses when the column was under fire, or when the way was lost and the guides were seeking the road, it would appear that the column was on the move at least eighteen hours out of the twenty-four, which would make its progress average a little over two miles an hour, or thirty-eight miles a day. This showing, while it is very good, would be much more creditable to the officers in command if the men and their horses had arrived at the end of their journey in good condition, which they most certainly did not.

The column made only a short halt at Malmani, and

pushed on for a few hours until 8 o'clock, when there was a halt of two hours and breakfast, and after that a short ride to Ottorshoop, a little town of corrugated zinc houses of one street. The rattling of machine guns and the tramping of hoofs brought the natives to their doors and windows, but with the exception of a constable, who rode off to warn the Commandant of Marico, into whose district they were now advancing, no one showed any alarm or interest at the invasion, but regarded them with the same calm curiosity they would have given to a performing bear or an itinerant musician. It was while they were passing through Ottorshoop that a young Englishman approached different officers in command, asking numerous questions as to the reason of their presence in the Transvaal, and concerning their future plans. He called himself "Captain" Thatcher, and said he had served in the "Guides," whoever they are, and volunteered for the expedition. His services were accepted by Col. Willoughby, who used him as a messenger. One of the younger officers to whom he had addressed some anxious questions told him to mind his own business, called him a spy and advised tying him up to a gun wheel until they reached Johannesburg. As it turned out this would have been an excellent precaution, as the youth ran away as soon as the force surrendered, and made his escape to London, where he posed as a hero, and by assuming to speak with authority, did the expedition as much harm with his silly speeches and bombastic newspaper articles as did the Boers with their rifles.

At Ottorshoop the telegraph wires leading to Zeerust and from there on to Pretoria were cut, thus shutting off the Boers for a time from any means of communication with the towns the column left in its wake. The wires running south to Kimberly and those to Johannesburg had already been cut several days before by Bechuanaland police, who had crossed the border in plain clothes for that purpose. From Ottorshoop the column moved along the southern slope of the Witwatersrand on the main road to Johannesburg, over a flat country, where only an occasional ranch showed above the un-broken line of the horizon. No one, either friend or enemy, appeared in sight, and with the exception of the Commandant of Marico, who rode out to meet them and to protest against their further progress, the day passed without incident. Jameson answered the commandant's formal protest with the following message, and allowed him to ride off unmolested:

SIR : I am in receipt of your protest of the above date, and have to inform you that I intend proceeding with my original plans, which have no hostile intentions against the people of the Transvaal, but we are here in reply to an invitation from the principal residents of the Rand, to assist them in their demand for justice and the ordinary rights of every citizen of a civilized state.
                                                            JAMESON.

For the remainder of the day the column moved rapidly along the Johannesburg road. The weather was fair, and the moon arose early, allowing them to continue on well into the night, when there was a halt of two hours, while the guards hunted for the road, only to find at last that they had never left it. So far the ride had been a pleasant picnic, and as peaceful as a prospecting party, and the long winding column, with its hooded carts and string of led horses and ranks of mounted men in their high boots and broad sombreros, and with bandoleers slung across their chests, must have made a picturesque contrast to the empty sea of high, waving grass and rolling plain about them. But no one took that point of view of their progress, and though they did not know it at the time, there was probably never in modern history 500 men who, while simply jogging across an imaginary line and over a wind-blown prairie, caused such great commotion in as many different and as distant parts of the world.

One gets an idea of how great this commotion was by re-reading the cablegrams that passed from Cape Town to London on the first peaceful day and during the three troubled ones that followed it. They were sent by presidents and prime ministers, and high commissioners and colonial secretaries, and in the wording of each, no matter from whom it came, you will find but one object, sometimes hidden and underlying the expressed meaning and sometimes roundly and openly set forth, and that one object is to show the writer's absolute repudiation of Dr. Jameson and of all his works.

It was most essential that they should make this clear. It was most important that the South African Republic, whose territory had been invaded, and all the rest of the world, should know that the great British Empire was not waging war upon that little state, and it was even more important to several individuals who were intimately associated with Dr. Jameson in other matters, that every one should understand that in this piece of lawlessness he played his hand alone, and without their sympathy or knowledge. But after one has read cablegram after cablegram, and message after message, and found nothing but shrieks of terror lest some one should suppose that the writer was in any way responsible for Dr. Jameson's conduct, the thing assumes an almost ludicrous aspect, and has a touch of the pathetic. Dr. Jameson was certainly an outlaw, and deserved no more sympathy than a common safe robber, but one does not expect the safe robber's pals to be the ones to throw the first stone. He did an exceedingly outrageous thing, and the consequences of his crime were far reaching and many. As the United States Ambassador to Rome said, in reply to an English diplomat, who asked him of what Jameson was guilty, and on what grounds he could be tried: "Well, you might begin with murder." All this can truly be laid to his discredit, but there is something to me vastly amusing in the sight of these many great dignitaries, prime ministers, high commissioners, presidents, dukes and Cabinet ministers standing huddled together, gathering their skirts around them and crying: "Please, I didn't do it: it wasn't me," and pointing frantically at this little band of mounted men fighting their way across the prairie. It reminds one of a room full of women standing on chairs and shrieking at a hunted, harassed and frightened mouse.

Sir Hercules Robinson, the High Commissioner of South Africa, was the first to put himself on record. He repudiated Dr. Jameson so quickly that his repudiation reached the gentleman before he was well on his way. Then the great British Empire, whose Queen had made Jameson a Commander of the Bath, filed its repudiation with resounding emphasis, and cast him off forever; then the British South Africa Company, Chartered, for which he had won Mashonaland, and who had made him its administrator, repudiated him and dismissed him from office. But all this, even had Jameson known of it, would not have convinced him greatly at the time, for he was in great difficulties, with retreat cut off and the way blocked before him, but it would certainly have added to the bitterness of his failure had he known that the Prime Minister of the Cape Colony had filed his repudiation, too. When the conspirators were stabbing at Caesar in the Senate Chamber, the blow that cut the deepest came last, and it came, as we all remember, from his friend. Jameson, as one of his messages shows, was prepared to be called a "pirate;" he knew that success was the only thing that could excuse his act, and that high officials must for their own protection turn against him, and yet he was the only one concerned who was in personal danger; he was the only one who was taking his life in his hands, and the figure he makes, riding through the storm of Wednesday night, with the darkness lit only by the flashes of the Boer's rifles, and reading in their light nothing but failure and disgrace on the morrow, is to me more attractive than the figure cut by these gentlemen seated comfortably at the Cape and in London board rooms denying him to reporters and washing their hands of their former friend. He certainly did upset the plans of Mr. Cecil Rhodes, and his conduct not unnaturally tried that gentleman's patience, but nevertheless it was not well of Mr. Rhodes to double on his tracks and join in the hue and cry after his old friend, and to shout,

"There he goes!   Stop thief!" even louder than the rest.

The exciting telegrams began tentatively with a cautiously worded one from the Colonial Secretary, Mr. Joseph Chamberlain, in London, to Sir Hercules Robinson, the High Commissioner of Great Britain in South Africa, at the Cape.   It was sent at 5.30 o'clock on Dec. 29, 1895, the same evening on which Jameson started.

To Sir Hercules Robinson:

(Strictly confidential.)   It has been suggested, although I do not think it probable, that an endeavor might be made to force matters at Johannesburg to a head by some one in the service of the company advancing from Bechuanaland Protectorate with police. Were this to be done, I should have to take action under articles 22 and 28 of the charter.*   Therefore, if necessary, but not otherwise, remind Rhodes of these articles, and intimate to him that in your opinion he would not have my support, and point out the consequences which would follow.   JOSEPH CHAMBERLAIN.

To which the unsuspecting Hercules Robinson, who, although at the Cape, knows less about what is going forward there than does Chamberlain in London, makes the following reassuring reply, the humor of which lies in the fact that it was received on the evening of Dec. 30, when Jameson had not only started, but was already many miles across the border.

To Mr. Joseph Chamberlain :

I learn on good authority movement at Johannesburg has collapsed; internal divisions have led to the complete collapse of the movement, and leaders of the National Union will now probably make the best terms they can with President Kruger.

Throughout the whole disturbance Sir Hercules Robinson behaved in a manner quite as absurd as his name, which name the English Government allowed him later to change for a title, probably because it was such an absurd name.   It is difficult to discover any other reason for elevating him to the peerage.   Sir Jacobus De Wet, Her Majesty's agent at Praetoria, was another gentleman whose conduct toward the Reform Committee was as odd as his name.   If Great Britain had many such representatives, her boundaries would soon inclose a country as large as Switzerland.

---

* The charter of the South African Company.

Mr. Chamberlain, who seems have been very correctly informed, was not entirely reassured by Robinson's answer to his first cablegram, as his second message shows. He wires:

To Sir Hercules Robinson:

Your telegram received. Are you sure Jameson has not moved in consequence of collapse ? See my cablegram of yesterday.

JOSEPH CHAMBERLAIN.

In reply to this Sir Hercules, who has at last awakened to what is going on about him, sends the following:

To Mr. Joseph Chamberlain:

Information reached me this morning that Dr. Jameson was preparing to start yesterday evening for Johannesburg with a force of police. I telegraphed at once as follows to the resident Commissioner in the Bechuanaland Protectorate: 'There is a rumor here that Dr. Jameson has entered the Transvaal with an armed force. Is this correct ? If it is, send a special messenger on a fast horse directing him to return at once. A copy of this telegram should be sent to the officers with him and they should be told that Her Majesty's Government repudiates this violation of the territory of a friendly state, and that they are rendering themselves liable to severe penalties.' If I hear from Newton that the police have entered the Transvaal, shall I inform President Kruger that Her Majesty's Government repudiates Jameson's action ?

An hour after this was forwarded to Chamberlain, a telegram was received by Robinson from Sir Jacobus De Wet, the British agent at Praetoria, the capital of the Dutch Republic.

To Sir Hercules Robinson:

Thirtieth December, very urgent. President South African Republican Republic sent for me and the General (General Joubert?) then read to us telegram from Landrost of Zeerust that a number of British troops have entered Transvaal Republic from Mafeking and cut the wire, and are now on the march to Johannesburg. I assured President that I could not believe the force consisted of British troops. The General then said they may be Mashonaland or Bechuanaland police, but he believes the information that a force had entered the State, and he said he would take immediate steps to stop their progress. His Honor requested me to ask your Excellency whether this force is composed of British troops or police under your Excellency's control, or whether you have any information of the movement ?

This last telegram from Praetoria was followed almost immediately by another verifying the first, and which is given here as part of one that Robinson sends to Chamberlain:

To Mr. Chamberlain:
Following further message just received from British agent, South African Republic.

Begins : Thirtieth December, most urgent. Commander general has received positive information that about eight hundred Mashonaland troops are close to Rustenberg, well armed with six Maxims and four other cannons, on march to Johannesburg, flying the English flag. His Honor desires me to say that an armed force of British subjects entering Transvaal Republic by force, is a serious breach of London convention, but he is much surprised that Her Majesty's government should allow such serious movements to go unchecked, and he still hopes your Excellency will take immediate steps to stop this force from proceeding any further, as His Honor cannot allow such encroachment on his legal rights with impunity, and most serious consequences will follow, for which his government cannot be held responsible. Awaiting immediate instructions. Ends.

I have instructed British agent to send at once a thoroughly trustworthy mounted express with following message from me to Dr. Jameson, to meet him on the road:

Begins: Her Majesty's goverment entirely disapprove your conduct in invading Transvaal with armed force, your action has been repudiated. You are ordered to retire at once from country, and will be held personally responsible for the consequences of your unauthorized and most improper proceeding. Ends.

The telegrams began now to fly like tennis balls across a net; all private messages were refused by the cable company, and the lines were kept entirely free for Government business. Mr. Chamberlain at the time made a very favorable impression by giving all cablegrams sent and received to the public at once, so showing that the Government was not responsible for Dr. Jameson's actions and was acting openly against him. Two hours after this cable arrived at the Colonial Office in London, another followed it at 12.30 o'clock on the 31st, by which time Jameson had accomplished nearly one-half of his journey without as yet having heard anything of these efforts that were being made to stop him. This telegram embodies another from Newton, the resident director at Mafeking, from which place, as it will be remembered, the Bechuanaland border police had started:

To Mr. Chamberlain:

In continuation of my telegram of this morning, I have received the following reply from Newton:

Begins: Thirtieth December. Your Excellency's of to-day. I have every reason to believe that the rumor to which Your Excellency refers is correct. Two troops of company's police left Mafeking last night, in an easterly direction, with two Maxims and two 7-pr guns. I understand the fact has been officially reported by the local authorities here to the Cape government. I received Your Excellency's telegram under reply in two portions, owing to an interruption on the wire, the latter portion arriving at 12:50, and at 1:30 orderly Sergeant White, Beuchanaland police, left here in plain clothes, with the best horse in camp, to overtake the force. I have forwarded a certified copy of Your Excellency's telegram to Dr. Jameson with a request that he will immediately reply with Your Excellency's instructions. I also sent a copy to the officer commanding the force, requesting him to circulate it among his officers, for their information and guidance. I also sent copy to the officer second in command and to the captain of the two troops from Mafeking. I doubt whether the messenger will be able to overtake the force within a hundred and twenty miles from here, as it probably had some forty miles start. As I understand, it passed through Malmani at five A. M. this morning. Any further information will be immediately forwarded to Your Excellency. Ends.

To this Chamberlain replies:

To Sir Hercules Robinson:

(Sent 2.10 P. M. 31st December, 1895.) You should represent to Mr. Rhodes the true character of Dr. Jameson's action in breaking into a foreign state, which is in friendly treaty relations with Her Majesty, in time of peace. It is an act of war, or rather of filibustering. If the government of the South African Republic had been overthrown, or had there been anarchy at Johannesburg, there might have been some shadow of excuse for this unprecedented act. If it can be proved that the British South African company set Dr. Jameson in motion, or were privy to his marauding action, Her Majesty's government would have to at once face a demand that the charter should be revoked and the corporation dissolved.

As your first messenger may not succeed in overtaking Dr. Jameson, and it is not impossible that the latter may disregard the message and even a second message sent by you to the British agent at Praetoria, could you not, with President Kruger's assent, send Sir J. De Wet himself to meet Dr. Jameson and order him in a still more authoritative manner to return ?

A day later, on Jan. 1, Sir Hercules received a second cable from Mr. Chamberlain, in which it is seen that nearly everybody playing in the cast has a fling at Jameson, repudiating him first singly and then all together in chorus:

To Sir Hercules Robinson:

Glad to hear of Rhodes' repudiation of Jameson, who must be mad. I see no need for Rhodes to resign. Telegraph direct to editors of papers in Johannesburg, Praetoria, and Bloemfontein that you, I, and Rhodes repudiate Jameson's action, and that you are commanded by Her Majesty to enjoin all her subjects in South Africa Republic to abstain from aiding, or countenancing Jameson or his force.

Her Majesty's government will repudiate Jameson's action publicly here. DeWet should, as you ordered Newton to do, communicate with each of Jameson's officers direct, telling those who belong to the regular or reserved forces, that they will be cashiered unless they obey Her Majesty's order to disarm and retire.

This next cablegram, sent the same day as the last from Robinson to Chamberlain, gives the *coup de grace* to Jameson, and makes all of South Africa repudiate him:

To Mr. Chamberlain:

Referring to your telegram of 31st of December I have asked De Wet to meet Jameson himself if possible, and to order him in an authoritative manner to retire. I have read your message to Rhodes and urged him to make a public disavowal of all complicity with Jameson. I believe his colleagues have given him the same advice. I have also impressed on him the necessity for his co-operation in directing Jameson's immediate return. I have seen a copy of a letter to Jameson, dated 20th December, from Messrs. Leonard, Frank Rhodes, Phillips, Hammond and Farrar, asking him to come to their assistance in case of disturbance in Johannesburg. I understand that these gentlemen now repudiate Jameson's action on the ground that the circumstances contemplated in their letter had not arisen when he started. Jameson's action is condemned all throughout South Africa. Not a voice is raised in his support.

The last line of this told what was absolutely false and absurd. Jameson could have had the aid of 20,000 men, could they have reached him in time, and had there been

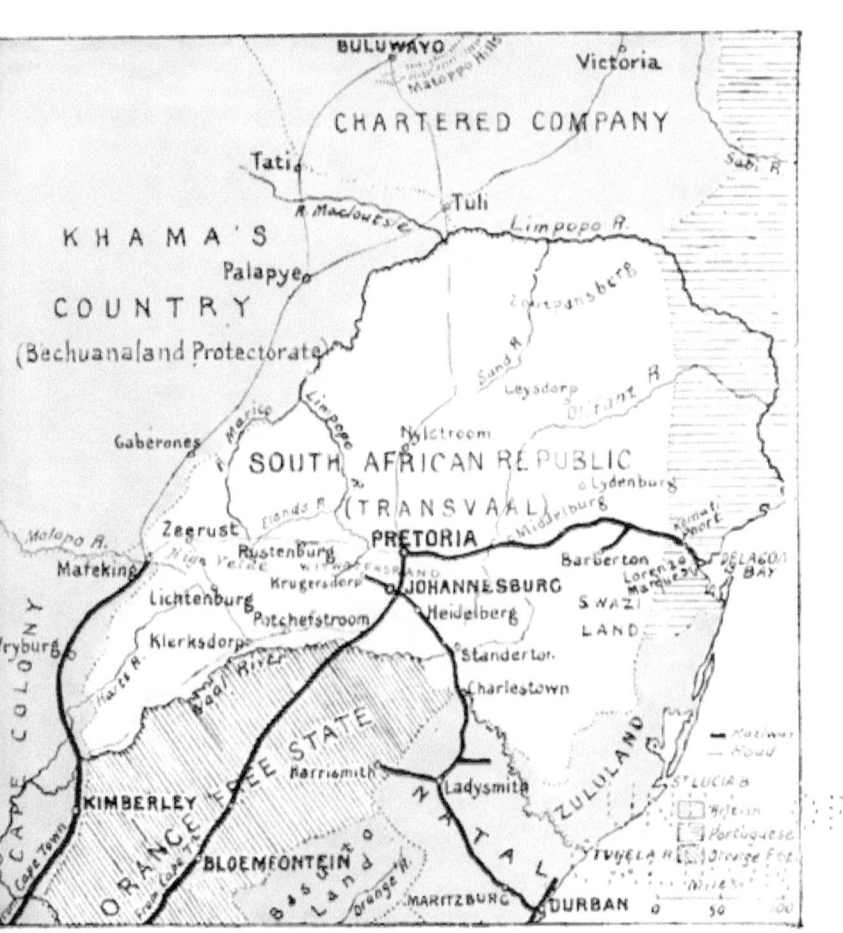

MAP OF THE SOUTH AFRICAN REPUBLIC

arms and horses for that number. So far from no voice being raised in his behalf, almost every city in South Africa, after his surrender, sent petitions to Praetoria, begging for his pardon and release, and he and his officers were cheered when they left the Praetoria jail at every railroad station on their way to the coast, and at every seaport town from Delegoa Bay to Aden, and by the troops ships in the Suez Canal, when the soldiers on their way to India swarmed up the rigging to look down upon the Doctor on the deck of the "Victoria." Not only the men, but women also raised their voices in his behalf, and the miners' wives waited for him five miles out of Johannesburg with bouquets of flowers, when they thought he was coming in. And in London ladies of high degree sat day after day in the courtroom at his trial, to lend him whatever influence there might be in great names and in great beauty.

While all this cabling was going on Dr. Jameson was riding rapidly onward, enjoying the peace of that first day and night on the veldt, which, as he probably suspected, was only the prelude of the storm to come.

His force halted at sunrise of the second day, Tuesday, the 31st, at a store where there were 300 horses waiting for them. The Boers had been told that a new stage line was being organized, and the presence of this unusual number of horses at one point had been explained to them in that way. But the new mounts proved of little value, and not more than half a dozen at the most were taken by the troopers in exchange for those with which they had started. There was another halt made about mid-day, but it was cut short by an alarm to the effect that the Burghers were coming, which proved to be false.

While the men were resaddling.Sergt. White, who had been sent after them from Mefeking, as described in the cablegram, rode into camp and delivered his letters to the different officers to whom they were addressed. The letters contained the telegrams sent by Sir Hercules Robinson to Her Majesty's agent at Mafeking. White had been furnished with two passes, one written in English and the other in German, but he had been stopped at Malmani by the Boers who read his letters, and then allowed him to proceed. The place at which he overtook Jameson was about ten miles beyond the Elands river, on the Johannesburg road. He delivered his letters to Col. Grey, who distributed them. Sir John Willoughby read his letter, and put it in his pocket, saying in answer that the matter would be attended to, and then gave the order to saddle and mount, and continued eastward. White rode back again, having overtaken the column eighty miles from Mafeking, although it had left that place eighteen hours before he did. He made the round trip of the 160 miles with one horse in fifty-two hours.

Dr. Jameson continued on without further interruption until 11 o'clock that night, when about 300 Boers appeared in the distance riding in circles and showing dimly in the moonlight. Both sides claimed that the other was the first to open fire, but that point in view of all that followed later does not seem to be of importance now. This was the beginning of the attack on the column, and with but few interruptions the remainder of the ride, which lasted thirty-two hours longer, was made under an almost constant fusilade. The Boers disappeared at daybreak, and at 6 o'clock the force halted for rest and breakfast. A little later it was met by Baur and Lace, two messengers from Sir Jacobus De Wet, at Praetoria, who had been instructed by the high commissioner to send some one out to meet Jameson, with a copy of the proclamation and with a message to him from the High Commissioner, ordering him to retire from Transvaal territory. A copy of this proclamation is given on the opposite page. It was published over all South Africa.

In answer to this message Dr. Jameson wrote the following reply, with which Baur and Lace returned to Praetoria. The message begins:

DEAR SIR : I am in receipt of the message you sent from His

JOHN HAYS HAMMOND

THE CAPE OF GOOD HOPE GOVERNMENT GAZETTE EXTRAORDINARY.

PUBLISHED BY AUTHORITY.

Tuesday, December 31, 1895

PROCLAMATION by His Excellency the Right Honourable Sir Hercules George Robert Robinson, Baronet, a member of Her Majesty's Most Honourable Privy Council, Knight Grand Cross of the Most Distinguished Order of Saint Michael and Saint George, Governor and Commander-in-Chief of Her Majesty's Colony of the Cape of Good Hope in South Africa, and of the Territories and Dependencies thereof, Governor of the Territory of British Bechuanaland, and Her Majesty's High Commissioner, &c., &c., &c.

Whereas it has come to my knowledge that certain British subjects, said to be under the leadership of Dr. Jameson, have violated the territory of the South African Republic, and have cut telegraph wires and done various other illegal acts;

And whereas the South African Republic is a friendly state in amity with Her Majesty's Government;

And whereas it is my desire to respect the independence of the said state;

Now, therefore, I do hereby command the said Dr. Jameson, and all persons accompanying him, to immediately retire from the Territory of the South African Republic on pain of the penalties attached to their illegal proceedings.

And I do further hereby call upon all British subjects in the South African Republic to abstain from giving the said Dr. Jameson any countenance or assistance in his armed violation of the territory of a friendly state.

GOD SAVE THE QUEEN.

Given under my hand and seal this 31st day of December, 1895.

(Signed) HERCULES ROBINSON,
High Commissioner.

By Command of His Excellency the High Commissioner,

(Signed) GRAHAM BOWER,
Imperial Secretary.

Excellency to me, the High Commissioner, and beg to reply, for His Excellency's information, that I should of course desire to obey his instructions. As I have a very large force of both men and horses to feed, and having finished all my supplies in the rear, must perforce proceed to Krugersdorp, or Johannesburg this morning for this purpose. At the same time, I must acknowledge, I am anxious to fulfill my promise on the petition of the principal residents on the Rand to come to the aid of my fellowmen in their extremity. I have molested no one, and have explained to all Dutchmen met that the above is my sole object, and that I shall desire at once to return to the Protectorate. I am, yours faithfully, (Signed) L. S. JAMESON.

The High Commissioner's orders, both to overtake Jameson and to head him off, had therefore been successfully carried out, but the result desired which depended on Jameson's obedience was, as has been shown, most unsatisfactory.

At mid-day two more messengers, who had ridden from Johannesburg on bicycles, met the column and gave Jameson a letter which they had brought from Col. Frank Rhodes, of the Reform Committee at Johannesburg.

This letter, a copy of which I have seen, but the exact wording of which I cannot now remember, began by saying that there must be some mistake, as there had been no massacre or disturbance at Johannesburg of any sort. It added that some of the Reformers had gone to Praetoria to make terms, and asked how the Doctor was coming along, concluding with the line: " I will have a drink with you when you get in this evening."

To this Jameson replied in another note, in which he said that he was coming in all right, and needed no help, but that if they could spare 200 men he would be glad if he would send them out to meet him, as they would cheer up his troopers, who were tired with their long ride.

This letter never reached Rhodes until three months later, as the messenger who carried it was stopped by the Boers on his way back to Johannesburg, and his machine was thrown into the shaft of one of the mines. He escaped from the Boers, and three months after the raid fished his machine out of the shaft and found the letter from Jameson, which he had hidden under the seat of his bicycle. It is now in the possession of Col. Rhodes. After the departure of the bicyclers, the column moved up within two miles of Krugersdorp, near the George and May mines, where its further progress was stopped by a party of Boers, who had fortified themselves in sluices and behind mounds of rubbish, which had been thrown up previously by prospectors when locating the gold ridges. The column at this point should have made a detour, and avoided the town altogether, or it should have risked the loss of a few men and pushed forward. Instead of doing this it wasted invaluable time by halting to shell the hiding places of the Boers, and also took unnecessary risk by advancing without cover into the fortified angle, which the prospectors had constructed apparently for the Boers' benefit and protection on that occasion. After two hours' firing the column drove the Boers back over a second hill, and destroyed two iron buildings behind which they had taken shelter. The fight while it lasted was watched from the George and May mines by a large crowd of workmen, who showed no other interest in the battle beyond that of curiosity.

Before opening fire with his field pieces, Col. Willoughby had sent a note to the Commandant of Krugersdorp, giving him notice of his purpose to shell the town if necessary, and warning him to remove all women and children to a place of safety. That was an act quite in accordance with usages of polite warfare, but as the gentleman says in the play, " What we want now is less etiquette and more hustle." The officers in command of the expedition must have known by that time that the only chance of its ultimate success lay entirely in their reaching Johannesburg before the Boers, who were assembling from every side, could combine and surround them in superior numbers. And instead of wasting time in unlimbering guns and shelling a few scattered men well hidden behind piles of rock, they should have

continued on at their best speed, and made for the open
prairie, where the Boers would have been in as exposed a
position as they were. Instead of which they worked
around to the right of the town, and so completely lost
their way that they were three hours in getting back to
it again. It was then about 6 o'clock in the evening, and
the rain was pouring heavily, the men were sick for
want of sleep and food, and the horses were jaded and almost useless. The troopers who believed in Dr. Jameson's promise of help from Johannesburg were accordingly delighted to see at that time a column of men to the
number of 400 advancing rapidly toward them. "Here
comes Frankie Rhodes," one of the officers cried, and
galloped forward to receive him, and was met when
within 300 yards of the approaching column by a volley
of bullets. The supposed reinforcements proved to be
Boers, who galloped toward the invaders so quickly
that the men had only time to fall off their horses and fire
a volley before they were well upon them. The fore-
most rank only saved itself by lying flat in the grass and
firing rapidly, while the Maxims were being run forward.
Col. Willoughby then formed his force into the shape of
a crescent, with the Maxims at the two ends. In this
position they fought for over an hour, when the Boers
having been forced back the centre withdrew, the left
and right flanks covering its retreat and drawing gradu-
ally together to fill the gap. The column then re-
formed, and moved off in the darkness, carrying five
wounded men on the gun carriages, and leaving three
officers and six men unaccounted for.

There are two roads by which the column could have
gone on from there to Johannesburg, the longer one is
to the south, and crosses the veldt, where one man is as
conspicuous a mark as another, and where the Boers
would have been forced to fight in the open. The second is the shorter way, and leads by deserted mines and
through valleys and by kopjes, which are great masses
of stone as high as a small hill. This latter road was
the one the Jameson officers, either through ignorance or

by trusting to Boer guides, as they are said to have done, selected to follow on Wednesday night. It led them into a virtual death trap. No one can blame a general, if while fighting in an unknown country, he stumbles into an ambuscade, but the Transvaal should not have been an unknown country to the Jameson men. They had been waiting idly on the border for six weeks doing nothing, and there was no excuse from a military point of view for their not having made themselves acquainted in that time with every inch of the road to Johannesburg, with every blade of fodder and every running stream and naturally fortified position on the way. The city is only 150 miles from Mafeking, and they should have been able to have walked to it blindfolded. Any one of these officers, were he going to ride a steeplechase, would take the trouble to walk over the course at least once, and the ignorance of all of those who conducted this expedition seems to me to be even a better reason for taking away their commissions than the fact of their having infringed a Foreign Enlistment act.

The night was very cold, and the rain still fell heavily; the men were wet to the skin, their stomachs were empty, their limbs were stiff and sore and their eyes so glazed for want of sleep that they could hardly see their gun sights. The Boer bullets fell among them from every side, and there was nothing at which they could fire in return but the flashes in the darkness. Toward midnight they lagged, and while half the force tried to sleep the remaining half continued firing, and many of those on guard took advantage of the darkness to steal away and desert the sinking ship while there was yet time for them to save themselves. One officer, who was sent out that night on patrol duty, told me that he had taken with him a detail of six men, but that only two reurned. He said the other four may have been shot, but he doubted it.

The raiders broke camp at 4 o'clock on Thursday morning, and moved to the right up the Langlaale road, which leads into the Dornkoop Valley. Two more men

had been killed during the night, and those who had
been wounded, with deserters, now brought the force
down to the number of 300 men. The rain had ceased,
and when the sun rose it shone down brilliantly on the
wet grass out of a blue sky. Those whose horses had
been shot were left behind and were made prisoners by
the Boers, who hovered far in the rear, and the ambulances had been abandoned at Krugersdorp.

The ride from this hour on became a rout. Men
threw away everything but their arms and ammunition,
and the track of the flying column was plainly marked
with discarded saddle bags and blankets and canteens,
and the little force which had been so magnificently
equipped on paper now rode forward stripped of everything but weapons, its riders bunched together and making a broad conspicuous mark on the rough highway.

It is no discredit to the Boers that they refused to give
fight in the open; as they were the challenged parties, it
was only just that they should have the choice of position
and of arms. They had not invited Dr. Jameson to a
fight; he had forced it upon them and they had a per-
fect right to protect their homes from invasion in whatever manner they found most effective. But it is only
fair to the invaders to point out that while they were
moving forward in regular order, as the nature of the
road required them to do, and making a target 200 yards
in length, their adversaries were hidden behind rocks and
ridges, firing at a very long range, and when they were
driven back galloping from one hiding place to another
under shelter of the hills.

The column reached the Stair Mine at 7 o'clock in
the morning and turned from it into the Doornkoop
valley, which was to be the valley of death to the Jameson expedition.

It was about eleven o'clock when Dr. Jameson
made his last stand. His position was at the base
of a huge kopje covered with boulders and stones,
which stretched out on either side of the advancing
column in the shape of a huge horseshoe. At the right

end of this horseshoe were two stone farmhouses, with
a stone fence at the back of them and a pool of dirty
water. The Boers occupied these houses before the column reached them, but were driven back by the Maxims
to the kopje, where they hid themselves, the Englishmen, in their turn, taking shelter behind the stone wall
and the nearest farmhouse. The invaders were now
caught in a triangle, and were under fire from three
sides. Had they reached the same point in their ride
three hours sooner, it is almost certain that they would
have gone safely into Johannesburg; for at the hour
when they did reach it the Boer artillery had not arrived,
and the Burghers themselves were only just appearing
over the horizon line. One of the men said it looked
as though they were springing from traps in the ground,
and that where there had been a dozen little specks on
the horizon there was a moment later 100 and then 200,
until wherever he looked he saw galloping figures, which
seemed to breed others as they came. The invaders,
now reduced to 294 men, were stretched out over a distance of a quarter of a mile.

Behind the field pieces the Chartered Company's men
stood in their greenish-gray tunics and bird's-eye puggarees, and the Bechuanaland police in brown karki and
white puggarees. The officers were in nondescript uni-
forms, chiefly the undress tunics of the Guards. Jameson wore a long driving coat and a soft felt hat, and
took no part in the attack, but watched it seated on his
horse, with a pair of field glasses, from a place in the
rear of the seven-pounders. Coventry, the only man
who caried a sword, was, in consequence, mistaken by
the Boers for the commander of the column, and was
selected by them as a special target.

The Boers used two Krupp guns and two Maxims
from behind the kopje, and the Staats Artillery, which
had arrived from Praetoria by special train, opened up
from the left, but did little beyond tearing up the earth
back of the stone wall. From where Jameson's men stood
they could see the derricks of the Rand rising to the

left, and the road to Johannesburg turning to the north
of the kopje. Grey sent Lieut. Grenfell, a nephew of
Gen. Sir Francis Grenfell, of Soudan fame, and two
men to reconnoitre the road and discover if it were possible to force a passage through it. One of the two
troopers was killed before they had gone a hundred
yards, and the bullets tore up the ground and splashed
on the stones around the horses' hoofs. Grenfell came
back, and reported that the way was impassable. Grey,
who had assumed command since Krugersdorp, where
Willoughby had been taken ill, looked over his shoulder
and saw the horizon line broken with rows of mounted
Boers, who cut off his retreat.

"It is the only way," he said. "We can't go back,
we must go forward."

"If three men can't get through there, three hundred
can," Grenfell answered.

Grey called 200 of the men together, and ordered
Major Hon. C. J. Coventry, the oldest son of the Earl
of Coventry, to charge the kopje and dislodge the Boers
by assault. It was the last desperate effort of the day,
and it was made with a sweep and a dash that would
have done credit to a noble cause. The men rode out in
skirmish line, the trumpets sounded and, led by Coventry,
waving the one sword, and Inspector W. H. Barry, they
charged for 400 yards to within 100 yards of the kopje,
and were met by a volley that knocked thirty men out of
their saddles. Barry was among these, and died a few
hours later.

But Coventry rallied them again, and they charged
once more, and were once more repulsed. As they re-
treated, Coventry let the line pass him, and rode behind
his men, looking back, and this time one of the bullets
found him and passed through his thigh, coming out in
front. He fell from his horse, with his foot in the stir-
rup, but the horse which he had ridden often before for-
tunately stood still, and he pulled himself up and back
into the saddle, and then fell forward on its neck and
called to his men to help. They rode back and lifted

him off, and laid him on the ground. His limbs were paralyzed from the waist down.

The firing from the Jameson column had slackened now, and the Maxims, as there was no water to cool the heated tubes, had jammed, and were silent. Gunners were sent to bring water from the pool back of the farmhouse, but it was raked by the fire from the Staats Artillery, and they could not reach it.

There was a hot, breathless pause, men were lying on the ground stretched out in strangely unfamiliar attitudes, dying horses were screaming and kicking up the earth, and the puffs of white smoke from the ring of rocks around the invaders showed them that over 1,500 rifles were turned upon them. They saw nothing to shoot at in return but these puffs of smoke. They were as helpless as men at the bottom of a well, and it seemed only a simple matter of time when each one of them would be eliminated from off the face of the earth, but they still continued firing, some sulkily, for they thought they had been betrayed; some crazily, for they were drunk for the want of sleep, and others with desperate courage. One trooper, who was wounded through both thighs and could not rise, dragged himself forward on his elbows, and placing his bandoleer before him, shot lying on his stomach, as coolly as though he were at the Bisley range. Another trooper, as though to shame the Boers for seeking protection, stood up in advance of the line and continued firing and cursing at the hidden enemy until two bullets passed through his lungs.

No one has told explicitly who it was that raised the white flag, or whether the order came from Jameson, Grey or Willoughby. There were two flags raised— one on the left and one which was placed over the stone farmhouse to the right, and it is interesting, as showing how difficult it is to write facts correctly, even when only a year has passed since they occurred, that three different men claim to have furnished the flag of surrender, one saying it was a torn shirt, another a piece of lint, and another his pocket handkerchief.

The flag was raised at 9 o'clock, or a few minutes after, and the firing, except on the extreme right of the line, instantly ceased. Messengers were sent to stop that firing, and after five minutes the Jameson force stood in absolute silence; but the Boers, doubtless through some error, continued firing for over fifteen minutes. Sir John Willoughby, who again assumed command after the surrender, sent the Hon. Henry White and Lieut. Grenfell to the Boer commandant in charge of the artillery with a note, asking him why he fired upon a flag of truce, and requesting to cease doing so.

The note in which Willoughby stated the conditions under which the surrender was made, was as follows:

"We surrender, providing you guarantee a safe conduct out of the country for every member of the force."

This note was given to Hans Klopper, one of the burghers under Commandant Potgieter, of the Krugersdorp District, who had ridden forward from the Boer lines as soon as the flag of truce had been raised. He either stopped on his way back and showed this note to Commandant Cronje, commandant of the Potchefstroom District, and the officer second in command of the Boer army under Gen. Joubert, or he was given two notes, for it is certain that both Cronje and Potgieter sent answers to a note of this import.

Potgieter's answer to Willoughby was to the effect that he would call a meeting of his brother commanders and consult them concerning the communication. But Cronje, without waiting to consult with any one, dispatched the following answer:

John Willoughby :

I acknowledge your note, and this serves as reply, that if you guarantee the payment of expenses which you have occasioned this South African Republic, and surrender your flag, together with your weapons, I will spare the life of you and yours. Please send reply within thirty minutes.   CRONJE.

This acceptance by Cronje of Willoughby's conditions shows the thrifty spirit of the Boers, but it is fair, and even generous, for Cronje's son had been dangerously

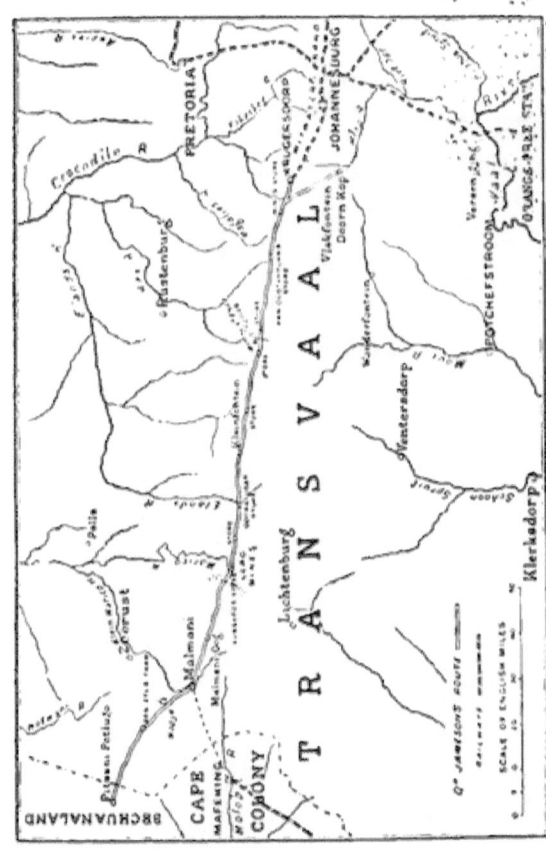

MAP SHOWING COURSE TAKEN BY Dr. JAMESON'S RAIDER

wounded by one of the Jameson force during the battle at Krugersdorp on the night previous.

Willoughby naturally agreed to these conditions, and fifteen minutes later sent a note in reply. He kept no copy of this note, but he says it was to the following effect:

I (or we) accept the terms on the guarantee that the lives of all will be spared. I now await your instructions as to how and where we are to lay down our arms. At the same time I would ask you to remember that my men have been without food for the last twenty-four hours. WILLOUGHBY.

The length of time which elapsed between the receipt and exchange of these notes is explained by the fact that those of the Boers nearest to the Jameson force were 500 yards distant, and many were 2,000 yards, or over a mile away.

What follows was at one time a disputed point between Jameson's officers and the Boer commanders. What the burghers say happened is this:

After receiving Willoughby's answer, Cronje rode up to where Jameson was standing by the stone farmhouse, and explained that he meant by the last clause in his note that he could only guarantee Jameson's life and that of his men until he handed them over to Gen. Joubert. He then asked him if, with that understanding, he was ready to lay down his arms and to give up his flag. Jameson replied that he had no flag, but Cronje, believing the invasion was part of a plot on the part of the British Government to seize the Republic Transvaal, asked him to swear to that fact. To this Jameson said:

"I declare upon oath that I have no flag."

Commandant Malan, of the Rustenberg District, then rode up to Cronje, who had already been joined by Commandant Potgieter and about thirty other burghers, and asked: "What is going on here? I also wish to know!" And Cronje told him that he had guaranteed the safety of Jameson and his men until Praetoria was reached.

To this Malan, according to his own account of the
surrender, said: "We cannot make any terms here. We
have not the power to do so. Jameson must surrender
unconditionally, and we can only guarantee his life until
he is delivered over by us into the hands of the commandant-general. Then he will have to submit to the
decision of the commandant-general and the Government." To this Potgieter answered: "I agree with
that." And Cronje said, "So be it, brothers." Their in-
terpreter was told to translate this to Jameson, who
bowed and taking off his hat stepped backward and said,
"I accept your terms," and ordered Willoughby to command the men to lay down their arms. The arms were
then laid down.

The Englishmen claim that at the time they laid down
their arms they did so on the conditions set forth in
Cronje's note, that they would be allowed to leave the
country unmolested if they paid an indemnity, and that
it was after they laid down their arms that Malan rode
up and refused to listen to this, declaring that they must
be taken prisoners to Praetoria without any guarantee
that their lives would be spared. The account the Boers
give of what happened, however, seems to be the correct version, the affidavits on this point of six or seven of
the Burghers all agree sufficiently to be convincing, and
disagree sufficiently to be even more convincing. They
show that each one of them is speaking from his own
recollection of the incident and not after consultation
with the others. The fact that Dr. Jameson bowed and
took off his hat to them, is stated by each of the commanders and in a way that shows it gave them a certain
simple satisfaction. The explanation of the difference as
to the terms of surrender is probably due to the fact that
although Cronje did write such a note as the one the
Englishmen agreed to, he exceeded his authority in doing so and his brother commanders were justified in repudiating it. In any event, an order which arrived a half
hour later from Gen. Joubert settled the matter finally, and
would have overruled any agreement made by a subordi-
nate.

It was sent in answer to a telegram to him from Commander Trichardt, who had telegraphed that his burghers were within 1,250 yards of the Jameson force, which had raised a white flag. Joubert's order was as follows:

"They must lay down their arms and surrender unconditionally. If not, then the firing proceeds. Give them not more than five minutes to decide whether they will surrender or not; otherwise the firing proceeds. Should they surrender, take everything in charge, bring them to Krugersville and the officers to Praetoria. Disarm them first."

As soon as Willoughby gave the order to disarm, the men threw themselves on the ground and some cried hysterically from disappointment and more probably from overwrought nerves, and others showed the exhausted state they were in by stretching out and falling into a deep sleep, as though nature refused to listen any longer to such idle questions as conditions of surrender or terms of imprisonment.

The burghers mixed freely with the invaders, and showed no signs of glorification, but acted soberly and with dignified generosity, feeding the half-starved invaders with their own rations and giving them water to drink from their water-bottles, saying that they were sorry they had had to shoot such young men.

This is the story of the Jameson raid, and it is, as I fully appreciate, a dry and matter-of-fact story, with the dramatic and picturesque side of the adventure omitted. But it seemed best to leave descriptive writing to those who took part in the invasion and who will some day tell what they actually saw, and to confine this account meanwhile entirely to those facts they have let drop. I have accordingly tried to tell only what happened, and not what it would be very easy for us to guess must have happened, under the conditions which we know existed during that four days' gallop. Dr. Jameson's act was suited to the buccaneering days of Sir Francis Drake. He tried to put back the hand of time some hundred and fifty years, but he only succeeded in jarring the works for a few seconds, and the hand swept him out of its way and moved steadily on.

His fate and that of his raiders is common history. They were taken as prisoners from the place of their surrender to Praetoria, where, after lying for some weeks in jail, they were pardoned by President Kruger and turned over to the custody of their own government and shipped home in the care of English officials, charged with having infringed the foreign enlistment act. On reaching London the rank and file were set at liberty, but the leaders of the expedition were tried on this charge, and, convictions having been found against seven of them, they were sent to Holloway Prison to serve out the following terms of imprisonment:

Dr. Jameson, fifteen months; Sir John Willoughby, ten months; Major Hon. Robert White, seven months; Colonel Raleigh Grey, Col. Hon. Henry White, Major Hon. Charles Coventry, five months each.

President Kruger's magnanimity in pardoning the men who had invaded his country was no less creditable to his heart than to his head. "Jameson dead," he said to a party of Boers who demanded that the Englishman should be led out and shot, "is worth nothing to anyone. With Jameson alive I can make any terms I please."

Throughout the whole disturbance in the Transvaal, Kruger showed himself more than able to cope with the three forces that contended together against him. He defeated the Jameson raiders in battle, he outplotted the revolutionists and he won a triumph of diplomacy over Mr. Joseph Chamberlain himself. If the right to rule is a divine right to-day, as it was supposed to be long ago, it would seem that in the bestowal of that right God is no respecter of persons. For the two rulers, who appear to rule by that right to-day, and who have outmatched the Empress of Great Britain and India, and the Emperor of Italy, both in diplomacy and in generosity, are an uncouth, unkempt farmer in South Africa and a half-naked king in the jungles of Abyssinia.

The story now returns to Johannesburg and the

Reformers, and explains what they did during the raid and why they did not go out to meet Jameson.

The first intimation that the people of Johannesburg received that Jameson had started was when they read of his having done so in the newspapers which came out on Monday afternoon, twenty-four hours after he had left Mafeking. The Government, at Pretoria, had, of course, heard of it at the same time, and at once sent a deputation down to Johannesburg, inviting the Reform Committee to send a deputation to Pretoria to meet the President and the Executive Council, and to consider what was to be done in the light of Dr. Jameson's invasion. The committee went to Pretoria, and there Lionel Phillips, as its chairman, offered himself and the rest of the deputation as hostages for Jameson and his force, if the Boers would allow them a safe conduct out of the Transvaal. At that time, it must be remembered, no news had been received of any hostile demonstration having been made by Jameson, or by the Boers against him. The joint deputations came to no decision, however, beyond agreeing to invite Sir Hercules Robinson to come from the Cape and act as mediator on the question of the grievances. The deputation from the Reform Committee then returned to Johannesburg to report what it had done. The position of the Reform Committee was now, owing to the precipitate action of Dr. Jameson in disobeying orders and in forcing them to show their hand, a most difficult one. They had, all told, about 1,000 rifles in the town, while the Boer Government had under arms and within call 8,000 burghers, each of whom was a fighting man. When Hammond asked Heyman, Dr. Jameson's military representative in Johannesburg, how long he thought they could hold out should they attempt to defend the town with the thousand rifles in their possession, Heyman answered, "About twenty minutes."

This, then, was the position in which Dr. Jameson had placed his friends and fellow-revolutionists. They were without arms to make a stand, and owing to his act

the fact that they had meant to do so was no longer a
secret, their purpose was exposed, and, as would-be
revolutionists, they were justly at the mercy of the Boer
Government.   On Tuesday night 1,400 more rifles were
smuggled hurriedly across the border, but in the confu-
sion which had continued from the moment it was known
that Jameson had precipitated the revolt, many of these
were lost, and many more were distributed to the wrong
people, and at least 500 fell into the hands of the Boers
themselves.   Those men who did not know how to ·
handle a gun were armed with what rifles there were,
and sent out into the streets to act as policemen, to protect the town from the Boers without, and from rioting
within, the Boer police having entirely withdrawn from
Johannesburg.

Another circumstance, which at the same time added
greatly to the difficulties of the Reform Committee, was
the fact that the inhabitants of Johannesburg knew that
they had invited Jameson to come to their assistance,
and they were now wondering why no preparations were
being made to meet him on his way, but the Reform
Committee knew, to its sorrow, that if it took the guns
away from its policemen and went to Jameson, it would
take every gun there was in the city out of it, leaving it
absolutely unprotected from the Boers, who were gathering in large bodies at different points surrounding Johannesburg.

But the people of the city did not know this, and the
Reform Committee could not tell them how helpless it
was without the Boers knowing it also, and at that time
almost their only safeguard against the Boers lay in the
fact that the Transvaal Government believed that there
were from 20,000 to 30,000 rifles hidden away in the town
of Johannesburg.

It was stated at the time of the raid by many different
people that Jameson had been promised a force of 2,000
men to meet him at Krugersdorp.   No such promise
was ever made to Jameson by the Reform Committee,
and, even had it been made, Jameson knew when he left

Pitsani that by coming in before his friends were armed he could not expect any assistance from them.

Nor, to be quite fair to both Jameson and the Reform Committee, did he expect such assistance, nor did the Reform Committee think he needed it.

One of Jameson's troopers reached Johannesburg early on Thursday morning at about the same time that Jameson was being surrounded at Doornkorp, and at once reported to Col. Rhodes and Hammond. The man said he had been sent on in advance by the doctor to tell them that he and his force were coming in easily, and would follow the messenger in "two hours," but that he wanted them to send a committee of citizens to meet him at the outskirts of the town in order that his act might not look like that of a something the name of which the trooper could not remember. Rhodes suggested "fillibuster" and "buccaneer," but the trooper shook his head until some one ventured "pirate," when he exclaimed: "Yes, that was the word." Rhodes laughed and said: "And I'll wager the doctor said d——d pirate." "Yes, sir, he did," the trooper answered, and then curled up, completely exhausted, under the table in the committee room, and slept there for five hours.

After this message was received, the committee was so confident that Jameson was coming in safely that the women of the town gathered flowers together and rode out along the highway to Krugersdorp to meet him and his conquering heroes. Another message from Jameson, which shows he did not expect any assistance, in spite of what statement he may have made to his men before starting, is the letter sent by him to Col. Rhodes in reply to the one brought him from Rhodes by the bicycler.

This message, in which he declares he is "coming in easily," and the one brought by the trooper who had left the column only five hours before the surrender, show that even at the eleventh hour Jameson had no idea but that he would ride straight into Johannesburg and was neither expecting aid or asking for it.

On the night previous to the surrender, when it was proposed in Johannesburg to go out and meet him, the Military Committee, whch was composed of Col. Rhodes, and Heyman, Frank White, and Jameson's brother, the last three being Jameson's own representatives in Johannesburg, the men who had been sent there by him to look after his interests, refused for an instant to entertain the idea that he needed help. Frank White had two brothers, Col., the Hon. Henry White and "Bobbie" White, serving under Jameson as officers, and Rhodes and Heyman were the doctor's oldest friends, and Jameson's own brother would naturally be supposed to take an interest in his welfare. But all of these men declared that sending a force to him meant leaving the city open for instant occupation by the Boers, and they insisted also that Jameson did not need help, even if it had been in their power to send it to him. They supposed, then, that he had with him 1,000 men, cannon, and three Maxims, and they thought that there were not more than 300 Boers between him and the city, and Frank White expressed the general opinion when he said, "The doctor is coming in with two columns of 500 men each, and he can walk through 10,000 Boers." This, then, is why the citizens of Johannesburg did not go out to meet Dr. Jameson.

In the first place, they had never intended to do so, nor had they ever made any promise to do so. It was Jameson who was coming to help them; and, in the second place, in spite of the fact that they had not guaranteed him any aid, even if they had thought that he needed it, they had no means of conveying it to him unless they chose at the same moment to hand the city over to their mutual enemy, the Boer. But what is more important to remember than all else besides is that there was no suspicion in the minds of any one in Johannesburg that Jameson was in need of assistance at any time during his ride.

As one of Jameson's officers expressed it to me in talking over the raid in London, "We thought," he said, "that we could go through the Transvaal like a Lord Mayor's show."

Many different reasons are given to explain why Jameson started when he did, against orders, knowing the helpless condition of Johannesburg, and with such an inadequate force, but the reason that probably is nearest the truth is suggested by a remark he made just before he rode out of Pitsani.

"Those men are funking it," he said. "I'm going to stir them up." That speech undoubtedly is the real explanation for his remarkable action. He wanted to play the part they had assigned him, and he thought the others were afraid to play theirs, and that the whole revolution would come to nothing. He wanted the acclaim which would follow his invasion of the Transvaal, and he thought that the chance of his doing so was slipping from him through the half-heartedness of the men of Johannesburg.

None of the men whose plans he wrecked assigns any motive to him other than the love of a fight, the desire to be in the centre of whatever is going forward, and the increased reputation that would have come to him. They describe him as a man who has no care for money. They say he could have made himself rich in Mashonaland had he wished to do so, and that in the daily routine of life he is unselfishness itself, but that in this case he failed because he undervalued his friends' strength and overvalued his own. The men whom he considered were "funking it" were in much greater danger for months than was Jameson during the three days of his ride. Their offer to go to jail as hostages for his safe conduct out of the country he had entered against their entreaties required much more courage on their part, knowing as they did that the Boers were only too anxious to get them there on any count, than it would have taken to have dashed across the veldt, gun in hand, to attempt an Adelphi melodrama rescue.

On the night Jameson was marched a prisoner to Praetoria the Reform Committee was all but lynched for not having gone to his rescue, and even then it could not tell the excited people that there were not over 1,500 guns in the whole city of Johannesburg. It was not until Jameson's brother stepped out on the balcony of the Gold Fields Building and assured the mob that he had been acquainted with all that was going forward during the ride, and that even had he known that his brother's life was at stake, he was satisfied that it would have been impossible to have helped him, that the people were quieted and dispersed. Three days later the Reform Committee was placed in jail, contrary to the promise made by Sir Jacobus De Wet, the agent of the English commission, that if it agreed to armistice it would not be molested. This promise he now denies having made. The matter will be finally cleared up when the Parlimentary committee meets this spring.

In the meanwhile, the testimony of Capt. J. F. Younghusband, as to the conduct of the Reform Committee after it went to jail is interesting as coming from one who was on the spot as a spectator only, and in no way interested in the revolution. In the *London Times* of May 2, he writes:

"And certainly of cowardice the four leaders cannot be accused, for I can show that they did not fear to face death, even in the terrible form to which they were sentenced two days ago. On one of those critical days after Jameson had surrendered they were told that the Boers were clamoring to have them seized and shot at once, and it was suggested to them that they should quietly slip away from the country while they still could. I was myself present on the occasion, and heard Col. Rhodes and Mr. George Farrar say at once that even if they were to be shot they at least intended like men to stay where they were. The others agreed with them, and, with one or two exceptions, the entire committee gave themselves up when the warrants were issued without any attempt to escape.

"May I therefore ask their countrymen to remove the stigma of cowardice which has been cast upon them?

To face any lawful punishment they are prepared. They did not flinch to face even death. But there in prison in a foreign land to have to bear the taunts of cowardice from their fellow-countrymen they feel is the cruelest blow that could be inflicted upon them—cruel to them and cruel to their children after them. And now, when the severest sentence that can by law be given has been pronounced against them, will not Englishmen show their justice by repealing the sentence of cowardice they so hastily passed upon Johannesburg and give the Reformers, in their hour of trouble the sympathy they deserve?"

There is one story of the Reformers which relates to Mr. Hammond and which was told me by others of the Reform Committee. Hammond was very ill during his imprisonment, and in consequence permitted to go to the Cape for his health under a heavy bail. He was at that time under sentence of fifteen years' imprisonment, and the bail was not so heavy as the fine he has still to pay, which amounts to $175,000. He did not give his parole to return to jail, and his failing to have done so would have meant nothing more than the forfeiture of his bail, the amount of which he could have very well afforded to have paid. And when he had once crossed the border of the Transvaal every man he met was his friend. He could on reaching the Cape have stepped upon the first out-bound steamer, and shaken the dust of the Transvaal from him forever.

"That is the last you will see of Jack Hammond," some one said to Kruger. "I think not," the President answered, "and even if Mr. Hammond would wish to escape, I know Mrs. Hammond, and she is too fine a woman to let him think of it." Two days before his leave had expired Hammond came back to Praetoria, and knocked at midnight at the door of the jail for admittance to what, for all he then knew, meant fifteen years of his life in prison, and the jailers were so amazed to see his face through the wicket that when he threw his valise, which he had carefully packed with whisky and cigars for his three fellow-prisoners, at one of them, the Boer picked it up without examining it and carried it to the cell which Hammond, Rhodes, Phillips and Farrar shared in common. Hammond had gained his temporary liberty because he was ill, and he would not take advantage of that act of kindness on the part of the Boers to fly the country, and so leave his fellow-conspirators to suffer a punishment which, if it was deserved by one, was deserved by all. It was a case of conscience, and of moral as well as physical courage.

When people accuse the Reform Committee of cowardice and of being men who failed to keep their word they should put before them these two pictures—the one of Jameson, surrounded by his 500 troopers, saying: "Those men at Johannesburg are funking it. I am going stir them up," and three days later raising the white flag; and the other of the American, Hammond, when still shaken with fever, he returned to serve out his sentence, and stood alone at midnight knocking for admittance at the gate of the Praetoria jail.

www.ingramcontent.com/pod-product-compliance
Lightning Source LLC
Chambersburg PA
CBHW022151020726
47496CB00008B/2661